Maisie's Escape

A short story from the world of
The Mark of the Artist

~~~

By Gina M. Engman
~~~

HUMAN
AUTHORED
Authors Guild
9238152

For E, N, & O.

Enjoy the adventure, kiddos.

"Kellogg, ya really shoulda used a better decoy. This one's not even as good as yer little girl." Chance Porter pointed at James. Chance was flanked by his crew, including the one with the bandaged hand and one with the remnants of the shiner Sebastian gave him.

Porter's man dropped a scrap of yellow cloth to the ground—it was a kerchief.

"She told me her papa would smash my head in when he found me," Chance Porter took a step forward. "Of course, that was after she stomped my foot and sucker punched Vergil here in the gut." Kellogg's eyes went very wide, but even in his fear there was a twinkle of pride. "So, Kellogg, think you'll be punchin' in my head tonight?"

He laughed. "Ah, my Maisie always was a keen one." He laughed again and cocked his head to the side—then swung his burlap sack round right into the side of Chance Porter's head.

~ The Mark of the Artist

She had lived here her whole life. Port City was home. That's all she knew.

Maisie Kellogg had seen it all, even by nine years old. She knew the places to hide, the people to run away from. She could find her way home from practically anywhere in the city. She knew the baker on St. Christopher's square added anise seeds to the bread on Thursdays, and that the washer women on Lang Street kept butterscotch for the kids who would deliver clean laundry bundles.

Maisie also knew the scum of the city. She knew to never go down Crabber's Lane, especially after dusk. The dock workers said it was haunted by the souls of old crabs eaten in stews, and you could hear their pincers click-clacking at sunset as they rose from the crevasses. Did she believe it? No. Maybe. But Maisie also knew that the Iron Key was on Crabber's Lane, among the empty old warehouses. There mighta been crabbers in some of them long ago, so better not go, just in case.

And the magical things—traders, villains, princes, and princesses waiting in the coffee house for their ships. Spices from far off mystical lands, and traders who ventured across the rough seas to find silks. At least that's what Papa told her. Papa had the best stories from the docks. He'd worked there since before she was born, and had seen more and talked to all the people.

Maisie loved it all.

She and Papa had a small flat upstairs of a wig maker, next to a cobbler's family. They didn't need much, as it was only the two of them. Mrs. Trent, the cobbler's wife, would let her stay with them on nights Papa worked late, which was a lot of the time. The Trent's had two sons, Vinny and little Simon.

Vinny was about her age but much taller and he was loud. Maisie was the opposite, keeping quiet most of the time except around Papa.

She wasn't short, not really, but for some reason the adults in her life thought of her as tiny. Decked out in her patchwork skirt, her blonde hair was bright like straw, golden and bouncy, and needing a brush most of the day. Papa said her Mama had hair just like hers, but she couldn't remember her.

On the nights Maisie stayed next door, Mrs. Trent would tell the children stories. Her favorite was the tale of the shoemaker and the elves. "Of course it is real! That was us, many years ago. Before you were born," she'd say to her boys. "How do you think we got all of this?"

Maisie's eyes would move across the shoemaker family's home. A squat flat like theirs, over their shop. Vinny and his brother shared a bed in a room with only a dresser and a few wooden blocks. The parents had their own small room with a bed and two other chests. The rest was one larger room with a potbelly stove, kitchen, table, and a few chairs scattered about. Her own was about the same size, she figured, though she didn't have to share her room.

If the story of the elves and the shoemaker was real, she'd thought, *then the Trent's should be living in a much nicer place.*

But, like usual, she said nothing and thought of it all in her mind. Vinny and Simon jumped around, talking about how famous they were to be in a fairy tale. Mrs. Trent would smile, giving all three another bun.

Even though it was obvious to her the story wasn't really about the neighbors, Maisie held on tight, deep down in her soul, to the dream of it. It could just be about someone else, someone far away from Port City. People came and went all the time here. It's a port, after all.

Like Uncle James. And Sketch. They came here from far away. When James and Sketch had come to Port City half a year ago she'd heard so much of their story. The best thing about being little was that people ignore you. It's simple to walk through a group of grown-ups while they play their guitars and dance and sing, talk with their loud voices. She'd done it so many times. Snuck up behind the group, picked up a glass and tried a sip of their ale. She'd spit it out each time since it turned her stomach. And Papa only caught her a few times. The other best thing was their tales.

When James and Sketch came to Port City, they'd gotten a job from Papa at the docks unloading and loading cargo onto ships.

"We're from out of town," James had said.

"Anywhere in particular?" Papa had asked.

"East," Sketch had replied.

"Uh huh," was all that Papa had said back. But Maisie had been sitting quietly on a box nearby instead of being in the schoolhouse and had heard the two new men talking before.

"Don't say anything about it. I'm done with it, James."

"You really believe your father's going to send someone looking? We haven't seen anyone so far."

"That's because we've kept moving. Like I said we should still do!" Sketch had started to get frustrated. She saw his face scrunch and his fist start to clench.

"With what money, Sebastian?" James had asked, throwing up his hands. "Those brigands took the last coins we had."

Sketch pulled a coin from his pocket, but Maisie could see it was wood and not real. He'd looked at it with a sad look on his face.

"Dammit, James, I realize that. Think I don't?" He had been starting to turn red in the face. "Just don't use my name, alright?"

"Then what the hell do I call you?" James had asked.

"I don't know. 'Your friend' maybe."

"Or 'sir'," James had mumbled.

She'd heard them talking about how Sebastian threw his paintbrush into a river when his mean papa and evil stepmother ran off his true love, just like in a fairy tale. Papa called mama his true love, but she was watching them from heaven now.

She loved to imagine what Sebastian's true love looked like. Sebastian didn't know, but Maisie had seen a picture of her once, only a drawing in charcoal he'd left on a crate on the docks. She'd hid behind it when playing hide and seek with Vinny. Whoever she was, she looked pretty, and tough; a fighter maybe, or a princess. Her eyes were wild and calm at the same time. Even though Maisie could tell Sebastian was a sad, heartbroken man, she thought he was nice.

Then there was James. Papa liked him, said he was a "kindred spirit." There was a kindness in James, like he could have been Papa's long-lost brother from across the sea. He had blonde hair like hers, and when they would take breaks at the docks, he would show her how to do sleight of hand tricks like pulling a coin from her ear or making a marble disappear. They came in handy when she and Vinny wanted to pinch stuff.

Uncle James told her that he and Sebastian used to steal pies from a kitchen where they'd grown up. But whenever she asked him to tell her where, he'd just say "east" like Sebastian did. Maisie had a feeling that James was running just as much as Sebastian was. Or, maybe more like searching for something; she wasn't sure.

And then there was the new man. Sketch called him his teacher. Uncle James called him Argento, which was a word she didn't know, but it sounded like magic. He was kind, like a grandpa.

"Excuse me, little one," he'd said to her one day as she and Vinny played in the street outside the coffee house. Vinny ran. Typical. Maisie only looked and said nothing.

"Thank you for waiting. I am looking for someone and my intuition tells me a young girl like you knows this city better than most of the adults think they do." She'd smiled at that. "Have you seen a man, dark hair, my height, possibly working as an…artist?"

The man had said that with mild hesitation. "He may be new to your city."

Maisie had thought about not telling him. Sebastian was scared that people were looking for him for his mean father. And she liked him, grumpy as he was. Plus, what if his true love was in danger and this man was after her, too?

"You think I mean him harm." It wasn't a question. Maisie nodded. "That is an intelligent thing to think. You are wise beyond your years." The grandpa took off his brown velveteen hat, dropping it to the ground. The old man squatted down, and Maisie took a step back.

"Please. Just a moment." He pulled a box from his bag and showed her what was inside. "He needs this back."

She craned her neck to see inside. The crowd of people around them didn't even seem to notice them. In the box was a paintbrush.

"He is an artist…" Maisie had whispered. The grandpa nodded, closed the box and stood again, rubbing his knees. On his shirt cuff was a button with a cow with wings. She'd laughed at the idea of flying cows.

"Sketch works with Papa and Uncle James on the docks." She told the grandpa, who smiled and nodded. "He's sad," she decided to tell him. "His true love is gone."

The grandpa put his velvet hat back on. "Perhaps I can help with that, too." He winked at Maisie. "Thank you, little one, for your help, and may I say your bravery." He offered her a peppermint from a small cloth bag. "You remind me of my granddaughter. She also likes yellow dresses." His voice had shuttered at the last part. Maisie had slowly taken the candy and darted off.

Papa had taught her a long time ago how to tell the bad people from the good. The grandpa Argento with the paintbrush was good. She knew it.

James and Sebastian were in the middle of an adventure, she had figured by then. And Maisie was about to have an adventure of her own.

Weeks later, after Papa and Maisie returned from visiting her auntie in the country for St. Christopher's, she was enjoying a bit of fun with Vinny. It was afternoon and the heat was radiating off the stone walls of the buildings. Papa and James were working, and Sebastian now spent much of his time at "the damned paint shop," as Uncle James called it. She planned to follow James there tomorrow and see this mysterious shop.

But today was the day the butcher stocked the jerky. Beef with a spice that melted in their mouths. Vinny and even Simon loved that jerky. So, they had a plan—stick ball.

Vinny and his little brother weren't very good at it, and she'd let them know. But Vinny'd won at Evens and Odds, so he got to throw. He stood on one side of the cobble stone street, Maisie on the other. Simon sat on a step nearby, close enough to yell at his big brother, far enough to avoid a punch.

"You're losing to a girl!" Simon teased and laughed.

"Shut up, stupid," Vinny snapped.

"Aim the ball already, Vinny!" Maisie waved her arms and nodded her head towards the butcher shop where a tray of jerky was sitting on the windowsill on display.

"I am!" Vinny yelled at Maisie.

"Ninny!"

"Sissy!" He yelled back at her, and hurled the ball across the street, aiming for that tray of jerky on display at the butchers. But Maisie was right—he wasn't good at this.

The ball missed and banged on a railing, bounced to the left, and slammed into a stone St. Christopher's Day statue still sitting out after the festival. The statue of the saint leaning next to a tall tree teetered and swayed and then tipped over. To the children, it fell slow like melting ice until it hit the cobbled street. Then off came the saint's arm and head.

"Oooohhhh you're gonna pay!" Vinny yelled.

"Me? You threw the ball!" Maisie shouted. The two argued as Simon ran away, deciding it was better not to be at the scene of the crime.

Loud shouts came from inside the building and the butcher poked his head out of the doorway. Maisie heard fast footfalls towards the front door of the home.

"Run!" Maisie yelled to Vinny, and they scattered. Maisie turned down an alley, hitching her skirt so she could run without tripping. Dashing over a few old crates, and some broken bottles, regular street trash, away she ran.

At the next street she veered to the left, going in the direction of the docks. Better to be near Papa than risk the wrath of the Butcher, or the statue owner.

Right as she made the turn someone grabbed her arm and yanked her back.

"Hey!" Maisie yelled. "Lemmie go!"

She was spun around and came face to face with two rough looking men. A quick glance and she knew these weren't Papa's friends. The one holding her arm chuckled way down in his throat, had a bushy mustache like an ugly walrus, and Maisie could see leftover crumbs still stuck in it. His partner was taller and lanky, and his shoulders shook as he snickered. She saw his eye had a light purple ring around it, like Simon got that time after Vinny punched him over a game of marbles.

"Not so fast, 'lil missy!" the first man sneered.

"Yeah, hold yer horses. We ain't gonna hurt ya." The second one with the shiner raised his eyebrows.

Maisie sneered back. She lifted her leg and stomped down hard on the walrus man's foot. Then she checked back and sucker punched the other guy in the stomach. He let out a sound like wind or someone getting sick. Each man stumbled back in surprise and pain as Maisie began to run again.

"Get her, Vergil!" the walrus man shouted. Recovering his breath and holding his stomach, Vergil took off after her. She was quick, but Vergil was tall and took long strides. In a blink Maisie was again held by the arm.

"My papa will smash yer head when he finds you!" Maisie shouted at the walrus man.

"Want me to gag her, Porter?" Vergil asked.

"I doubt it'll work on a little brat like this," he replied.

She kicked and yelled but the man held her tight around the stomach, like a parcel being delivered.

"Stop it!" she shouted. Her heart was racing and she heard it pumping in her ears. She kept squirming to get loose, but the one called Virgil held on.

"Shut up," he whispered, and she smelled old onions in his breath.

"You stink! My papa will smash you!"

"Yeah, you said that before, brat," Porter said and grabbed her yellow kerchief from her head.

"Hey, gimmie that back, it's mine!" Maisie clawed and scratched at him.

"I'm gonna give it to your papa. Then he'll know you're with us, brat," Porter sneered.

Maisie's face puckered into a growling sneer. She even let out a low growl. She saw Porter glance at her but kept on moving.

"If you give my Papa my kerchief, then he'll really punch you good, you slimy walrus man!"

She knew it wasn't her best, but between being shoved and kicking and looking to see where they were, Maisie's mind was running in circles.

"I'm scared," Porter mocked, and put his fist to his mouth.

The men rounded the corner, Maisie still being carried like a sack of flour under Virgil's arm. That's when she saw it—the faded street sign tacked to the building: Crabber's Lane.

"Oh blazes!" she whispered, but they didn't hear over their own heavy footfalls. She searched the gutters as they passed for ghost crabs and listened for the click-snap of haunted pincers. They scurried past the Iron Key, locked up dark and tight for the night. All around was the smell of rotted fish.

Why didn't they cover my eyes if they're kidnapping me? she thought. *Stupids.*

Next thing she knew, they had pushed through a door and went inside a building. Virgil half dropped, half put her down onto the floor, and she sat against a wall. The room was empty except for some tables and a toppled-over chair. A lantern glowed on a window ledge.

"Hey you!" Porter was yelling at someone else. A voice sighed from around the corner.

"Are you addressing me?"

A man came out from around the corner of a wall, from some other room. Maisie supposed it was the kitchen since he was holding a bottle of some liquid. He was slender and moved like a person who normally would be quick, but because of a sloshed up head, now took great control not to fall flat on his face. He was a mess; his green velvet vest was miss-buttoned and missing some of the shine it could have had. Red hair stood out on the sides of his face from under a similarly ratty green velvet hat, sitting sideways on his head also as if it could tip right off with one wrong step.

"I prefer to be called by my name," the new man continued. "A name as they say is one's greatest asset! I am Javier Goodfellow. Peddler of wonders, purveyor of parcels, spreader of trinkets—"

"Drinker of whiskey," Virgil snickered. Goodfellow shot the henchman an evil look, but went on.

"He who can find the mystery in the ordinary. The epic in the dull. I who have held the Orb of Sanity of the great wizard of Glasgow."

"Too bad ya don't have that blinkin' orb now," Virgil muttered.

"A 'course, a 'course, oh bringer of mystical thingamabobs. How about you instead bring us some rope?" Porter sneered.

"Rope? Why ask me? I, who traveled the great plains of icy Norway only to capture a stone from the collection of the Helsinki fiord dwarves. Ask that other fellow with the bandaged hand, Porter." Goodfellow waved his hand about, looking around the room absently, and took a swig from his bottle. Maisie watched as he staggered closer to them and raised her eyebrow. He smelled like bad ale and mold...and lies. "Where is your friend?" Goodfellow glanced around.

"We'll meet him there," Vergil muttered, stamping his foot and shaking his finger to stop Maisie as she tried to slip towards the door. "Nice try, little miss."

"Get down there," Porter barked.

There was a hatch in the floor down to what she figured was the basement. Maisie froze.

"Make me, walrus man."

"Stupid girl." The two men picked her up under her arms and took her to the hatch. Goodfellow followed. The group shuffled down the staircase into the basement. It was muggy and more like a dank root cellar that stank of potatoes and dirt. Maisie wiggled and squirmed as they put her on a splintery chair. Virgil, the smelly one, tied her hands behind her back and her legs to the chair, all the time breathing out onions.

"Now what you have to say?" He chuckled in her face.

"You stink," she said, "and Papa will break your head."

"Ahggg."

Porter slapped Goodfellow on his shoulder, who snorted as he seemed to wake up. "Watch her. She's our bargaining chip. We'll be back soon with the silver." Goodfellow made a mock bow and waved his hand in a courtly manner.

Chance Porter turned to Maisie. "Gotta go meet your Papa."

Darn that walrus man, Maisie thought as she screwed up her face into a crooked scowl. *Papa will crack his head for sure.*

Goodfellow took another wooden chair over to the foot of the stairs. Maisie watched as he plopped down into the chair, almost slipping off the front. A part of her felt sorry for him. There was a sadness in this man's face, aside from the drink, that spoke of a loss she could feel. She watched as his chin dropped slowly down to his chest.

Cellars were nothing to be scared of to Maisie. The rooms Papa and she live in next to the shoemaker's shop had a large cellar they shared. It was full of shoemaking things, and smelled of leather and oils. She and Vinny hid down there on hot days, even if it stank of fish and old leather. At least they'd be cool. But this one was colder than that one, even on this hot summer day, and she wished she still had her kerchief on. The floor was damp and laid with large flat stones that were brown like hides.

Across the large room were a stack of crates, some covered with grayish canvas tarps, like most basements. Thick wooden beans spanned the ceiling, holding up the planks of the floor above. And she heard a drip. It reminded her of the drainpipe outside her window on rainy days.

The drip of water tricking down the bricks typically would drive a person crazy in this situation. But not Maisie. She sat and wondered out loud. "Where's that water comin' from? Is it from a wash basin that tipped? Did that once, Papa was mad, it ruined some of his things. Maybe it's from a bucket with a small hole at the bottom and it's spilling across the wood floor up there and will make green mold grow on these here bricks. All slimy and then you'll end up with bugs. Big red ones that like to live in the bottom corners of the basement in Mrs. Wolden's schoolhouse. They crawl all over down there. I saw a bunch go runnin' off when Vinny and me snuck down there with his mama's lantern. Vinny stomped about ten of them and this yellow creamy stuff came out and—"

"Shut up!" Goodfellow yelled. "Just shut your trap!"

Darn this stupid liar guy, Maisie thought as she screwed up her face into a crooked scowl. *Wish I could see Papa crack his head, too.*

She wiggled against the ropes on her hands and legs. The chair was old and rough and if it weren't for her long patchwork skirt her legs would have splinters in them.

It felt like she'd been down in the basement for hours, and she might have. It was hard to tell. The sun was down for sure, and moonlight was starting to come in through a half-moon window at the street level. Maisie almost wished one of the first two men had stayed behind to watch her instead of this Goodfellow man. At least then she could remind them how she'd punched them.

"What kinda name is Goodfellow?" she asked.

The man lifted up his head and looked at her. A few times he cocked his head side to side, like a slow bird attempting to think hard on something. "Have you not heard of me?"

Maisie shook her head. "Nope."

"Degenerate child," Goodfellow slurred the end of his words. "I am Javier Goodfellow! Peddler of wonders, purveyor of parcels, spreader of trinkets—"

"Ya said that before," Maisie interrupted. "But you don't seem like a good fellow to me."

"My name is Goodfellow."

"Is it a joke?"

"No! It is my name! 'Goodfellow!'"

"But good fellows don't kidnap little girls."

He opened his mouth to keep arguing, but stopped. Maisie fluttered her eyes and they stared at each other. He let out a sound between exhaustion and sickness. He took a swig from a brown bottle of something that smelled a lot like old ale.

"I'm thirsty," she said.

"You had water an hour ago."

"I'm hungry."

"Well, which is it?" he demanded through clenched teeth.

"Both."

"Dammit!"

"You shouldn't swear."

"I shall swear if I so choose!" He removed his hat and scratched his head. His dingy red hair stuck out at the sides and looked like it hadn't been washed in weeks.

"Fine. I'll get you some food. There must be something upstairs. But that's it." He rose from his chair and swayed on his feet.

"And water," she added.

"Errr. Fine. Then you shut your mouth!"

"Then how do I drink?" Maisie's eyes twinkled.

"Ahhhh!" the man growled as he staggered to the stairs.

"Thank you!" she called sweetly after him. "You smelly ass," she muttered under her breath and giggled at her own word choice.

The second Goodfellow was gone, she pulled her hands out of the ropes and freed her legs.

These guys really aren't dock men like papa or they'd have tied the rope right, she thought as she shoved the rope into her pocket.

Maisie scooted off the chair and darted to the other side of the cavernous room and ducked behind the stack of crates. Next to them were some moldy barrels. She smelled the old wine mustiness even before she read the words stamped on them: Rum, whiskey, and vino. She knew that meant wine, even though it smelled like vinegar. When you grow up on the docks, you learn things.

Beside the barrels was a door in the wooden wall, covered halfway by another canvas tarp that hung down like a curtain against the wall. Most of this part of Port City was built as rows of warehouses, modified over the years into shops and still held old secrets. Maisie knew most of them, but not here on Crabber's Lane.

She fished a tool from her pocket. It was a small ring with two metal sticks the length of a man's finger. Uncle James called it a lock pick. He'd shown it to her at the beach the other week after she'd found some buns in a picnic basket. Papa had been upset about her taking the buns, but had eaten one anyway. She knew he didn't like it when she pinched things, reminded him too much of himself, she'd heard him say to James that day.

But she knew Papa loves his Maisie-girl.

For a second, Maisie started to sniffle and she caught herself. She wanted to cry, and felt tears welling up in her eyes. Where is Papa? Shouldn't he be coming for her? It's nighttime and she could see the moon now through the half-circle window. Maybe Papa's punching that jerk Porter!

"Papa," she whispered. But now wasn't the time. Better get out and warn Papa of these jerks.

Keeping low behind the crates, she popped her head up only for a moment to make sure Goodfellow was still upstairs. Pick in hand, she bent over to the small door and pulled back the white tarp hanging in the way. With her pick, she fiddled with the lock listening to the clicks—Uncle James' lock picker worked way better than her hairpins! Suddenly, a final click, and the door popped open a crack. As Goodfellow's footfalls started at the top of the stairs, she slipped through the door.

Just like the room she was leaving, this cellar floor was covered in large flat brown stones. It wasn't damp though, like it was taken care of. She crept in the through the door hatch, then stood at her full height of almost four feet.

Above were the same thick wooden beams holding up the floor, which made sense since it was all one big building.

That was when Maisie jumped.

"What was that?" she said out loud. "A owl? In here?" She slowly turned around and saw it—a giant painting sitting against the wall, from floor to ceiling. Two lit lanterns glowed on either side sitting on propped up crates, casting golden light on the painting and the room. A castle stood high on a hillside, next to a flowing river of night. Dark and mysterious trees to one side, like an enchanted forest. The blue-purple night sky with the shimmer of thin clouds and glimmer of a pale moon. One light lit up the castle tower's lone window. Her eyes were drawn to its glow.

"Oooo…" she sighed. "Like a princess castle." Maisie took a few steps towards the painting. She saw the gentle brush lines the closer her nose came to the canvas. Some were thicker paints of darker colors, looked like they'd been slapped on. Others were short strokes and lines, some dots. She took a few steps back to look at the whole painting. "So pretty," she whispered. "Like that tale Papa tells about the evil witch and fancy princess waiting around for a prince to rescue her." She paused. "I wouldn't wait."

And she didn't. She heard loud voices outside on the street and knew Goodfellow would be back by now. Even a drunk smelly guy would notice she wasn't in the chair! She checked the door hatch behind her to make sure it was closed tight, then ran past the beautiful castle painting. She swore she heard the river, but no, it must be the sound of the waves at the docks.

This cellar also had a staircase, and she started up it two at a time, hiking her patchwork skirt up to her knees so she could dash with a rush of yellow. At the top of the stair was only a hole reaching the next floor.

The smell reminded her of the oils on the docks but with a cleaner scent. A set of odd-looking crates were stacked in the back, most with bright colors painted on different sides, which Maisie had never seen at the docks before. There was an easel with a painter's canvas set up. A faint outline of three oak trees and a bonfire was sketched with charcoal. She paused and stared. It reminded her of the small square painting Sebastian had handed her at the docks a few weeks ago.

"This for me?" she'd asked, the small painting in her hands. It was a piece of a wooden box, cut down into a small square. She'd gazed at the picture of a woodland—deep green leaves, tall dark trees, a red mushroom. Specks of yellow and white dotted the trees.

"Sure kid," he'd said. "You like it?" His question had sounded a little hesitant, like he wasn't sure it was really any good. She couldn't understand why.

"Yes! Thanks, Sketch! I love it, can't wait to show Vinny, he'll be so peeved I own art and he doesn't!" She'd laughed and scampered off. Maisie thought about later that night, when she'd put the small square on the table, leaned up against the wall. As she fell asleep she dreamed of the sound of tinkling bells, like fairies in the night.

"Sebastian must love painting in this place. I wonder if he'll let me come back here?" she whispered to herself as she realized quickly it had to be his. She crept through his art studio and into another low-lit room.

The next main room of the shop stopped her cold. Only a lantern at a table was lit, so she knew someone had been there recently. It was full of paintings. Every wall hung so many. She couldn't believe it.

Even with her heart racing to move she passed so many bright colors and pretty things. And they were mysterious, too.

One had a tree that looked like a face. And a house with the shadow of a man on the roof. That one creeped her some and she moved by.

Another was so beautiful. A girl, or woman, she corrected herself, posing to be painted. In her hand was a carved walking stick and a yellow headband the same color as her own favorite kerchief. Maisie picked up a small stool so she could look closer. So many pretty little details.

The woman was sitting like a princess but her clothes were much like Maisie's own, patched in places and well worn. She had long brown hair that curled in places around her face. "Wait…" she whispered. "You're her! You're Sebastian's true love!" It was so obvious now to Maisie that it had to be her, she had the same eyes as the charcoal sketch she'd seen him leave on the crate at the docks. This version of her was much better, but the eyes!

Behind the woman was a scene from a storybook. Maisie counted all the things: a church on a hill in clouds, a small cart going along a road, a port with buildings and a bay just like here in Port City. She saw grapes on the princess's walking stick, and a large tree like the ones on St. Christopher's day icons.

As she looked more at the beautiful painting she thought, *Wonder if she was a princess? She looks like she didn't wait around either.* She giggled.

A loud crash from next door shook her attention and she stumbled off the stool landing hard on her backside.

"Dammit!" she blurted, then caught herself and put her hand to her mouth, looking side to side as if someone could have heard.

"Where the hell is she?" a man yelled from next door.

"Gotta go," she whispered and made for the front door of the shop. Hesitating only to peek back at the princess in yellow, she smiled. "No, you didn't wait around, and me neither!"

Maisie scampered out onto Crabber's Lane, not listening for ghost crabs, white-blonde hair glowing against the wooden buildings.

"I'm coming, Papa!" She called out into the night as she ran.

Acknowledgements

One of the greatest joys in being a Mom *and* a self-published author is the sweet pride that my kiddos have for my writings. To them, I'm just the same as those who wrote the books they find at the library. And they aren't shy about telling people. "My Mom is an author!" "It's the best book ever!" "Read my Auntie's book!" (I'm also a proud Auntie.) It makes my heart sing.

But then one day my daughter asked a question about my book *The Mark of the Artist* that I just couldn't answer! As I was telling her the story, with some modifications for her age, she asked: "How'd Maisie escape her kidnappers?" I sat there, mouth open, stumbling around for an answer and I had none. "She just did, I guess" was the best I could come up with.

I started to think more about Maisie and what might have happened to her—how this spunky, smart, sly nine-year-old girl would handle being kidnapped by oafish brutes.

And now you know. I hope you have enjoyed her story!

Thank you as always to my best friend and husband, Walter, for supporting my dream of being a "real" writer. Also, thank you to my buddy-writer A.M. Dunnewin for switching up our writer-coffees to writer/kiddo crazy dinners!

And thank you to my kiddos. This is for you! I love you guys.

Chapter 1

The church bell tolled the hour—six brisk chimes rang across the town square. The white church steeple popped its head a bit above the low orange tiled rooftops of the tiny village.

Spring had finally come to this part of the country and all the window boxes were full of colorful tulips, daisies, and marigolds. Nasturtiums draped down from high windows and crept along sunny walls. A large rose bush blossomed in a wooden barrel in front of the Sow's Ear tavern. The tavern owner's wife planted it many years ago, though the bright pink roses did not quite match the clientele of an alehouse as the owner complained regularly, not that his wife cared two shakes what a bunch of ale-soaked rowdies thought of her beautiful delicate flowers.

The town began to wake. Wooden shutters swung open letting in the warm morning sunlight. At the bakery, sweet buns are laid on the windowsill to entice passers-by, the smell of sugar and lavender spreads across the square. Mr. Howard, the farmer, shouts at a group of boys who bolt in front of his wagon, heavily laden with the latest crop of beans and peas ready for market. The good children skip to school in blue caps and red checkered aprons, faces scrubbed and lunches tied in handkerchiefs.

The bells stirred pigeons and doves from their nests in eves of the church, so they flock together on the cobblestones of the square, shuffling around the fountain searching for their breakfast.

Sylvia watched the little birds from her seat at the fountain, tossing them bits and crumbs of the lavender bun.

Her sheep were done being watered, but morning brings such a bustle, one she never sees on the hillside with her sheep, that Sylvia lingered a moment on the fountain edge watching as more of the townsfolk stroll into town. A farmer's wife carried eggs to market while her friend gossiped about someone named Muriel. The two women laughed out loud as they passed the young shepherdess. A loud *Clang!* resounded through the square—the blacksmith starting his work.

Caroline, the town seamstress, opened her door and swept remnants of red thread onto the cobblestone street. Her dress was a magnificent emerald green with gold brocade, nothing like the shabby brown tunic and dingy white apron Sylvia wore. Caroline waved and called out to the farmer's wife. The women smiled and exchanged pleasantries. Then the seamstress turned back to enter her shop—her dress twirled around her, catching the sunlight and sparkling.

Something about the sight of the swirly green fabric made her sigh, so Sylvia stood and started to shuffle the sheep towards the north of town—out to the grazing fields of Mr. Albright, husband of the grand Mrs. Caroline Albright. Mr. Albright owned much of the land around the town, but has allowed Caroline to keep her shop since she loved it so much—at least that's what they told people. Truth was women from across the county come to buy dresses made by Mrs. Albright, allowing their husbands to pay a visit to Mr. Albright, making the couple quite rich. Funny what you learn being a part time housekeeper—and part time shepherdess.

Before Sylvia could get the sheep in order she noticed a bright cart bumping along the north road. The cherry-colored cart was drawn by an old mule, and sitting atop the driver's seat was a man with bright red hair. He was wearing a velvet green jacket and a matching top hat. The peddler circled the fountain slowly and finally stopped the cart near the bakery, where everyone must pass.

The peddler hopped deftly down from the driver's seat of the cherry-colored cart. He shuffled about and unfolded the side of the cart to display his wares. As the driver scurried about, a few of the townsfolk began to gather, whispering to one another about the strange red cart and the stranger man.

Before the whispering townsfolk could decide what to think, the peddler jumped up on a small platform and bellowed, "Good people! I, Javier Goodfellow, peddler of wonders, purveyor of parcels, spreader of trinkets, invite you all to peruse these wares. Behold!" He flicked his hand and a panel dropped on the right. Inside the hidden compartment was an onyx chest no more than a foot long and studded with rubies. "This once belonged to the Magistrate of Bulgaria. It is said to contain the writings of the Magistrate's chief wizard, but, alas, I have not had the courage to pry it open and see the wizard's writings myself." The peddler cast a downward glance and shook his long red hair.

"Good people!" he shouted again, looking up. "In the East, there is a magical land of gold and light called Shangri-La. There, in a castle of diamonds is a golden king who rules with a steady hand and a gracious countenance. Many people have searched for this fabled place and many more have lost their lives in that search. But I, Javier Goodfellow, have seen this land with my own eyes!"

The townsfolk squeezed in closer. The baker and blacksmith, who had been whispering near the rear, now moved to the front.

"After spending many nights in this glorious place, the Golden King sent me on my way and gave me this statue to remember my time in his kingdom." The peddler waved his hand and a panel on the left slipped away revealing a small golden statue of a chubby smiling man. The figure sat cross-legged and held his hands out to the side with fingers touching. *Ooo's* and *ahh's* murmured from the crowd.

"Ah yes, what an elegant king he was." Goodfellow nodded pensively.

The people broke into chattering as a man dressed in a bright green overcoat walked into the crowd. Murmurs of "Morning, Mr. Albright" chimed from the townsfolk, and the blacksmith stepped aside, allowing the man to pass to the front.

The peddler watched this obvious display of deference to the newcomer. The man was average height and going bald, which he tried to cover with a fluffy comb over. But his clothes were finely made and he had a gold chain strung from a pocket, which the peddler assumed went to a just as finely made golden watch.

A younger woman in a fine green dress came to the balding man's side and he kissed her cheek. She was younger than him, but not enough to be a daughter.

"Good People!" Goodfellow called, grasping a golden rope. "Behind this curtain is perhaps the most enchanting item I've come across in my many years of travel. As I traveled through the mountains in Spain, I came across a band of gypsies who invited me into their camp. I was leery, for all know that gypsies cannot be trusted. But I was weary and in need of food, so I entered the gypsy camp. Around the fire the women danced—in a brazen manor, I tell you." He nodded to a group of elderly women who had gathered to hear this strange man's tale. "And the men played on pipes and lutes. As I watched the gypsy revelries, an old woman approached me. She took my hand and moved her finger on my palm." He spread his arm to the crowd in demonstration. "Her wizened face grew dim and she squinted. Then, just as quietly as she approached, she rose and drifted way in the darkness.

"In the morning, the gypsy band was gone, leaving nothing but the charred wood of the last night's fire. But in my hand is what you are about to see, good people." He paused and glanced side to side, eyeing the crowd. Then, *whoosh*! The curtain was pulled back and on a green velvet pillow was a ring of shining copper. Though small, the metal caught the morning sun and reflected it into the crowd. More *ooo's* and *ahh's* floated up from the townsfolk.

"I cannot say what this ring means, but surely the old gypsy woman left it because of its power. Why else would I wake to find it in the same palm she had read the night prior?"

The villagers nodded and agreed. Sylvia stood on tip-toe from the back of the crowd, but glanced back to her sheep when something yellow moved out the corner of her eye. The man in the green overcoat stroked his beard in affected contemplation.

"So come, good people, and see the other treasures Javier Goodfellow has to offer." The peddler jumped down from his platform and swiftly set up a table covered in the same green velvet, where he set out his trinkets. There was a ruby ring worn by the Count of Copenhagen before his beheading, for carousing with the mayor's daughter no less. He had a belt of woven brown leather once worn by a Roman centurion. Next was a large silver punchbowl marked with odd symbols Goodfellow found while trekking in the Alps. Though he could not confirm it, a goatherd told him it was the drinking goblet of a giant. The blacksmith paid forty-five for the bowl. He had whalebone dice won from stranded pirates that the tavern owner bought for ten, an ebony paintbrush Goodfellow bought from a monk in Italy, and a brass key said to unlock the door to Avalon, if it could ever be found.

The townsfolk bought dolls and tarnished utensils, satin pillows and leather-bound books. Goodfellow gladly told the origins of each item he sold, almost sad to part with them for such reasonable prices, but what is a traveling trader to do?

The man in the green waistcoat watched from the side as people made their purchases. "You, my good man, are wondering how much for the cloak," Goodfellow called out to him. The peddler motioned to a bright sea-green cloak hanging next to the ebony box of the Bulgarian Magistrate. The cloak had intricate gold brocade stitching, and the back was embroidered with a field of gold stars.

"You would like it for your…wife? The lovely young woman there." Goodfellow pointed to Caroline Albright who was perusing the wares with some of the local women.

"Quite right," Albright said in a low voice. "Her birthday is in two weeks."

"Well, if I may be so bold, sir, this cloak would be a wonderful addition to the lady's wardrobe. And for two-fifty it is quite a deal." Albright seemed unenthusiastic. "This cloak was worn by the Princess of Algiers when she rode her horse to meet her new bridegroom in Istanbul. And, I was told, it was blessed by a holy man to bring prosperity to her marriage."

"Hmm," Albright said in an obvious attempt to sound unimpressed, but Goodfellow saw he'd already made the sale.

"Tell you what, my good man, I will also part with this paintbrush along with the cloak. It was once used by a rogue master painter of the Florentine court."

Albright picked up the brush. It was quite sturdy but felt lithe, and was carved with an intricate design of vines.

"Many ladies these days are learning to paint, I'm told," Goodfellow added.

"Ah, not my Caroline," Albright handed back the paintbrush. "My wife is a seamstress, quite talented, and enjoys that as her pastime—not that she needs to work, mind you."

"No, of course, sir," Goodfellow responded correctly. He laid the paintbrush next to a shiny oriental lamp and turned back to the other patrons. "That vase was sculpted in Greece, see the image of the dragon," the peddler explained to the florist who had picked up the pearly white vase.

"Wait!" Albright called. He looked at the paintbrush and the cloak. "I will give you no more than one-fifty."

Goodfellow laughed. "I'm sorry, my good man, but that is impossible. For the cloak alone I can go no lower than two hundred." He turned back to the florist.

"I will give you two hundred but I want the paintbrush as well," Albright said smugly. The peddler paused and glanced at the cloak.

"That, sir, is highway robbery. But as it will soon be your lady's birthday, I will do it for two."

"And the brush?"

"Yes, sir, and the brush." Goodfellow and Albright shook hands. "You strike a hard bargain, sir."

Albright smiled, pulling out his purse as the peddler wrapped up the cloak and brush.

By the time the noon bells rang across the square, Javier Goodfellow was five miles south of the town, his dead uncle's mule plodding along, cart bumping along the road, shipwreck-scavenged trinkets swinging back and forth from leather holders.

The Mark of the Artist

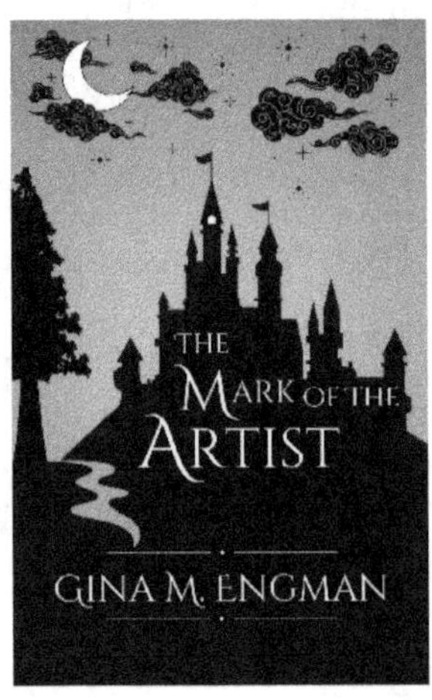

Art has power.

Sebastian Albright is realizing how to wield that power...on the other side of the painting.

The Artist's paintings are beautiful, enchanting, and ever so real. Churning blue waves crashing on a rocky shore—so real you can hear the waves. To his father and stepmother, Sebastian is nothing more than a road to wealth and fame.

Anna, the strange and beautiful servant in her patched yellow dress, sent away for rumors she was a traveling gypsy, and for getting too close to Sebastian. Only Anna knew what Sebastian's art meant to him. She had been the person who saw through his temper and façade and saw the Artist for who he truly was. And now she was gone.

Sebastian attempts to escape his old life and broken heart in a city near the sea with his best friend, James—a good man with secrets of his own. Instead, Sebastian encounters a silver-haired old man calling himself Argento. This man's own paintings are masterful and eerie, hinting at something more than just beauty and truth. Argento convinces Sebastian not to deny who he is—an Artist.

With the encouragement of his mysterious mentor, Sebastian creates a mystical masterpiece—a castle in the moonlight, blue and haunting, with a flag on the tower bearing a harlequin pattern of red, white, and black. And in the tower window is a woman: Anna, the one who had stolen the Artist's heart.

Is Anna *really* in danger, held prisoner by a madman known as the Harlequin Man, as Argento tries to convince them? Is Sebastian ready to embrace his talents and create a way to get to her—on the other side of the painting?

About the Author

Gina M. Engman grew up reading everything from classic novels and fairy tales, to science fiction and fantasy. She loves the hero's journey, myths, and legends. Art, symbolism, poetry, and the spark of hidden meaning drove her to become a writer, with *The Mark of the Artist* being her debut novel.

When not writing, you can find Gina enjoying the Sacramento, California sun with her beloved husband and two amazing children.